SHINE
AND THE
CHAOS CREW

The Day of the
HOWLING HEAD TEACHER

Written by Chris Callaghan

Illustrated by Amit Tayal

Collins

Shinoy and the Chaos Crew

When Shinoy downloads the Chaos Crew app on his phone, a glitch in the system gives him the power to summon his TV heroes into his world.

With the team on board, Shinoy can figure out what dastardly plans the red-eyed S.N.A.I.R., a Super Nasty Artificial Intelligent Robot, has come up with, and save the day.

Shinoy was on his way to Maths, when he was shoved from behind.

It was his super-strict head teacher, Mr Amitri, and he was running along the corridor holding a small green rucksack.

"Give it back!" A girl from Reception was running after him.

"Come and get it!" Mr Amitri laughed.

Mr Amitri skidded to a halt.

 "TOAST!" he shouted, then he disappeared into the main hall.

Shinoy watched him race around, stealing toast from the Breakfast Club.

It was hilarious. It was also really weird, and when really weird things happened, there was only one thing to do. "Call to Action, Chaos Crew!"

Shinoy activated the app on his phone. From a flash of light, the fierce warrior Salama appeared.

Shinoy grabbed a coat hanging up near
the piano and handed it to her. She groaned at
its pink softness but understood she needed
a disguise.

"Can I help you?" asked Mrs Button,
the school administrator.

"No. I will help you," said Salama.
"I will fight all evil."

"This is Ms Salama," explained Shinoy, "a … er … school inspector."

"I'll get you a cup of tea. Do you take anything in it?" asked Mrs Button.

Salama growled, "The tears of my enemies."

"I think we only have semi-skimmed milk, but I'll have a look." Mrs Button ran off.

"What foe must we defeat today?" Salama asked.

"It's the head teacher," explained Shinoy.

"Let us vanquish him!"

"I don't want him vanquished!"

Salama turned to see Mr Amitri trying to catch a fly in his mouth.

"Is this whom you speak of?" she asked.

Shinoy nodded.

Mr Amitri shouted to the stunned kitchen staff, "Let's chase each other around the playground!"

The staff didn't look keen.

"We need to get him away from the non-combat humans," whispered Salama.

Shinoy picked up a leftover piece of toast. "Mr Amitri? Would you like this?"

Mr Amitri licked his lips and followed. It was enough to tempt him all the way to the head teacher's office.

Mr Amitri plonked himself into
his chair, panting.

Shinoy recognised some of his
Maths homework on the desk – it had
been half eaten. He'd spent ages on that!

"Something's not right," said Shinoy.
"He's usually grumpier than my dad on
bin night."

"A Mind Belt will identify the problem," said Salama, holding a long black strap.

"You think he's had his mind swapped? Like Merit in series 1?"

"It is wise to assume the worst," replied Salama.

Shinoy offered to fix the belt around
Mr Amitri's head, thinking Salama might
struggle with her one arm. Losing an arm
in battle didn't stop Salama from being
amazing, but it did cause minor difficulties.

Suddenly, there was a knock on the door.

"Enter if you dare!" Salama roared.

"Mr Am—" It was Toby, holding his Maths homework.

He looked at them fixing the Mind Belt to Mr Amitri's head.

"That's a detention right there," said Toby.

"Mind swap," explained Shinoy.

"Ooh, nice. I'm staying to see this."

Mr Amitri tried to lick his own nose.

"He's much more fun like this!" laughed Shinoy.

"But what about the luckless fool who has the mind of your Teaching Master?" Salama said.

"Good point," Shinoy said.

Suddenly, Mrs Button appeared holding a cup of tea. Her mouth dropped open.

"It's a new part of the inspection," said Shinoy. Salama and Toby nodded.

"I see," said Mrs Button. "No tears, I'm afraid, but I found biscuits."

Mr Amitri pounced and gobbled them in one mouthful.

"I'll get more," she said, shuffling out backwards.

"It is as I feared –" Salama said, "complete mind swap, worthy of our enemy S.N.A.I.R. The other mind is in this room."

There was a noise from a cupboard.

"Brace yourselves for attack!" Salama warned.

Shinoy grabbed a plastic ruler. Toby stood behind Shinoy.

Salama opened the cupboard door, but there was no attack. It was the school dog, who growled angrily!

"He's so cute!" said Mr Amitri. There was a familiar, furious look in the dog's eyes which reminded Shinoy of Mr Amitri.

They attached another Mind Belt to the puppy, and Salama began to reverse the mind swap.

The puppy's tail started wagging.

"Eh? What? Who?" muttered Mr Amitri.

The dog jumped on to his lap and licked his face.

"The inspection has been a success!" announced Salama.

"Inspection?" squeaked Mr Amitri.

"Yes! And a warrior dog for the school is an excellent idea."

"Um, well," Mr Amitri spluttered. "His name's Eddy – short for Education."

Shinoy groaned – his head teacher was back to normal.

As Salama left, she winked. "Never fear, the mind swap was not totally successful."

Brain game

Ideas for reading

Written by Clare Dowdall, PhD
Lecturer and Primary Literacy Consultant

Reading objectives

- make inferences on the basis of what is being said and done
- answer and ask questions
- predict what might happen on the basis of what has been read so far
- explain and discuss their understanding of books, poems and other material, both those that they listen to and those that they read for themselves.

Spoken language objectives

- ask relevant questions to extend their understanding and knowledge
- participate in discussions, presentations, performances and debates

Curriculum links: PSHE: Living in the wider world – what rules are; Shared responsibilities and communities – different roles; Keeping safe – rules

Word count: 836

Interest words: activated, foe, vanquish, non-combat, assume, detention, luckless, mind swap

Resources: paper and pencils, outline of Salama, voice recorder

Build a context for reading

- Look at the front cover and read the title. Ask children to suggest why a head teacher might howl.
- Read the blurb with the children to find out about what will happen in the story. Recall school rules that are sometimes broken.
- Ask children to discuss what a *fierce warrior* is and to describe the characteristics of any that they know from other stories.

Understand and apply reading strategies

- Read pp2–3 together. Ask children to explain what is unusual about Mr Amitri, the head teacher's, behaviour.
- Challenge children to suggest what has happened to Mr Amitri to make him break the school rules.